P9-DDC-112

BEN CLANTON

Atheneum Books for Young Readers
New York London Toronto Sydney New Delhi

For Theo!

The cutest in the world!

atheneum

ATHENEUM BOOKS FOR YOUNG READERS

An imprint of Simon & Schuster Children's Publishing Division

1230 Avenue of the Americas, New York, New York 10020

Book design by Ben Clanton

The text for this book was set in Typewrither.

The illustrations for this book were made using watercolors, colored pencils, potato stamps, and digital collage.

Manufactured in China

0917 SCP

First Edition

2 4 6 8 10 9 7 5 3 1

Library of Congress Cataloging-in-Publication Data

Names: Clanton, Ben, 1988– author, illustrator.

Title: Rot, the cutest in the world! / Ben Clanton.

Description: First edition. | New York : Atheneum Books for Young Readers, [2018] | Summary: Rot, a mutant potato, enters a "Cutest in the World" contest but worries when he sees his competition.

Identifiers: LCCN 2016058146 | ISBN 9781481467629 (hardcover) | ISBN 9781481467636 (eBook)

Subjects: | CYAC: Beauty, Personal—Fiction. | Contests—Fiction. | Self-esteem—Fiction. | Potatoes—Fiction. | Humorous stories.

Classification: LCC PZ7.C52923 Rot 2018 | DDC [E]—dc23

LC record available at https://lccn.loc.gov/2016058146

This is Rot.

He's a mutant potato.

Like most mutant potatoes, Rot loves . . .

and **ALL** sorts of **GAMES** and **CONTESTS**.

So when Rot sees a sign that says CUTEST IN THE WORLD CONTEST, he can't wait to enter.

CUTEST
in the
WORLD
CONTEST
ENTER NOW!
THIS WAY!

Rot is sure he'll win.
He is so sure, he sings
a winning song.

I'm the
WORLD!
in the
cutest
in the

Cutest in the
The CUTEST
WORLD! The
Cutest CUTEST
WORLD!!!
CONTESTANTS LINE UP HERE
My EARS! My POOR EARS!
WHAT is that AWFUL SOUND?

But then Rot sees the other contestants.

There is an
itty-bitty baby bunny
with fluffy floppy
ears,
a little-wittle
bewitching
bewhiskered
cuddly kitten,
AND an eenie-weenie
pink and peppy
jolly jellyfish.

The other contestants don't think much of Rot's chances.

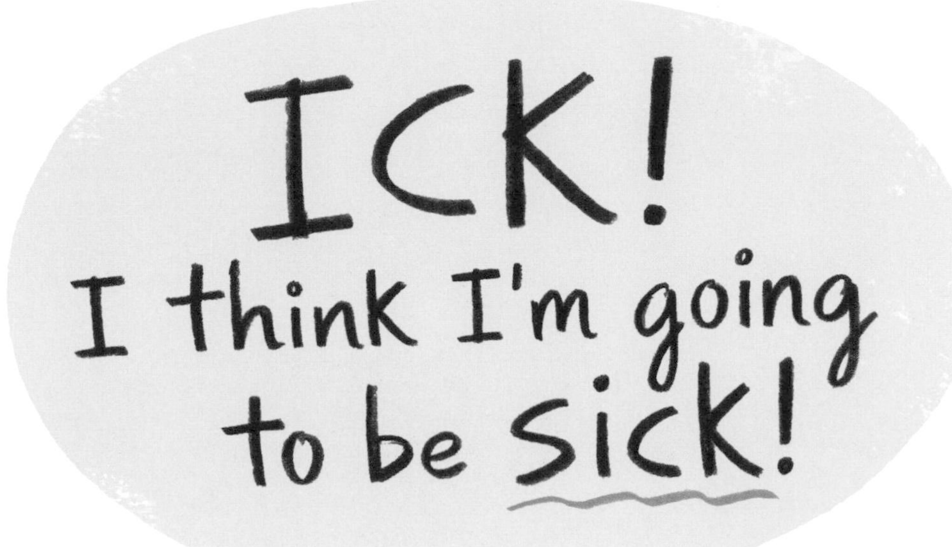
ICK!
I think I'm going to be SICK!

Whoa!

Rot considers eating everyone. He would win for sure if he were the only contestant.

But it wouldn't be a very nice thing to do and would probably give him indigestion.

Maybe Rot would be cuter
if he had BIG EARS like the bunny?

LOOK! I LOOK LIKE YOU!
Um...no.

Or maybe it would help
if he had whiskers like the kitten?

They're kind of ITCHY!
You look RIDICULOUS! Take those off!

Perhaps if he were pink and peppy
like the jellyfish?

We're PINK
and we're happy...

None of it makes Rot
feel any cuter.

So Rot decides to just be himself.

He doesn't stand a chance!

Is he actually going up there?

That takes guts!

LAST UP, ROT!
STAGE

Rot steps
onstage
and struts
his stuff.

He smiles his BIGGEST smile!

He shows his best side!

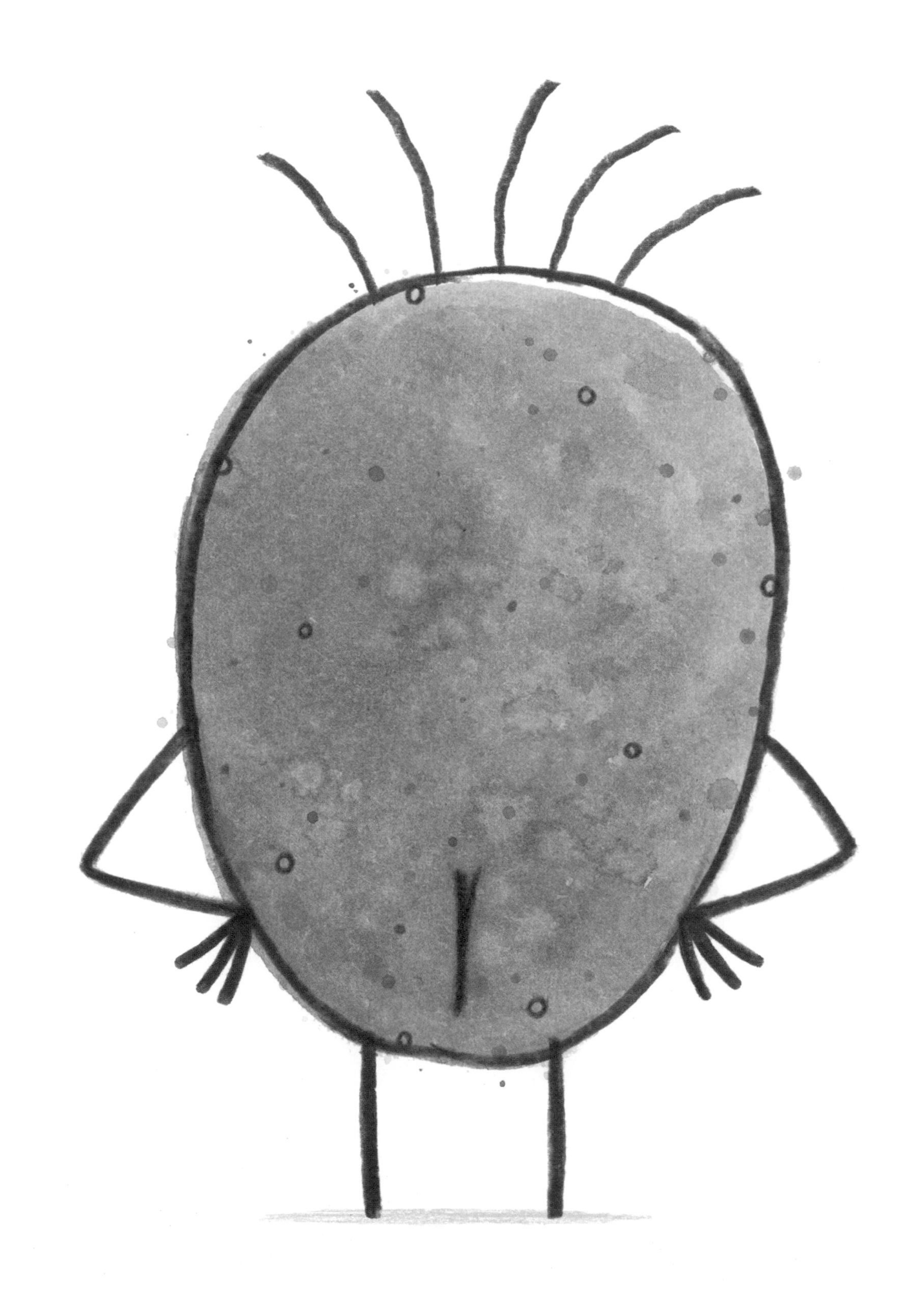

What do the judges think?
(DRUMROLL, PLEASE!)

Whisper
Whisper

ROT is the CUT
in the WO
I think I'm in LOVE!

HE'S PEAR-FECT!!!

Seriously?!
No way!
Huh!

Rot gets a GREAT BIG TROPHY.

It is so shiny that Rot
can see his reflection.
And Rot thinks he
looks like . . .

The Cutest in
Ugh!
This contest was totally RIGGED! WAIT... are you wearing a unibrow?
Um... do you like it?

the WORLD!

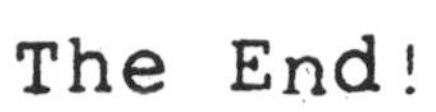

The End!